The Smurfs are getting ready for Smurfette's surprise birthday party! Can you find these smurf-tastic treats?

HAPPY SMURFDAY SMURFETTE

Gargamel is performing one of his sold-out magic shows. Look for these magical wonders of Gargamel the Great.

Gargamel needs Smurfette to give him Papa Smurf's magic formula so he can turn Vexy and Hackus into Smurfs. Can you find these things in his suite?

Patrick, Grace, Blue, Victor, and the Smurfs arrive in France, ready to rescue Smurfette. Do you see these things on the streets of Paris?

Eiffel Tower snow globe

Baguette

Hazelnut crepe

Beret

French flag

Mime

When Hackus is cornered in the candy store, Smurfette and Vexy come to the rescue! Can you find these smurfalicious sweets around the shop?

Gargamel tries to win Smurfette's trust through kindness. As he treats her to a ride on the Ferris wheel, find these pals who are searching for her.

© Peyo

Patrick and the Smurfs find Smurfette just in time! Search Gargamel's underground lair for these things he planned to use in his formula.

The Smurfs celebrate the safe return of their smurftastic friends! Do you see these Smurfs at the party?

Return to Smurf Village and smurf 20 gifts for Smurfette.

Levitate back to Gargamel the Great's magic show to find these audience members who have been transformed.

Join the Smurfs on the streets of Paris and find these blue things that catch their eyes.

Check back into Gargamel's suite in Paris to find these books that Gargamel has been studying in his quest for world domination.

Return to the candy store to find these Smurf-shaped sweets.

Smurf back to the park to find these sculptures.

Go back to Gargamel's underground lair to look for these failed potions that Gargamel created.

Take a portal back to Smurf Village to find Smurfs playing these instruments.

© Peyo